BOOK CLUB EDITION

Donald Duck and the Magic Stick

Random House New York

 Published in the United States by Random House, Inc., New York, and simultaneously in Canada by Random House of Canada Limited, Toronto.

Library of Congress Cataloging in Publication Data

Disney (Walt) Productions. Donald Duck and the magic stick. (Disney's wonderful world of reading, #26) With the help of his magic stick Louie retrieves Huey's magic table and Dewey's magic donkey and proves to Uncle Donald that there is such a thing as magic. [1. Fairy tales] I. Title. PZ8.D632Do [E] 74-16493 ISBN 0-394-82564-0 ISBN 0-394-92564-5 (lib. bdg.)

Manufactured in the United States of America 1 2 3 4 5 6 7 8 9 0

C D E F G H I J K

7 8

Once upon a time there was a tailor who lived with his three nephews.

The poor tailor worked very hard, while his nephews spent all their time playing and sleeping.

One day the tailor decided it was time for Huey, Dewey, and Louie to go to work.

"You must learn how to take care of yourselves," he said. "I cannot always look after you."

The next morning the three nephews left home.

"I will go to the city," said Huey.

"I will go to the country," said Dewey.

"I will go to the woods," said Louie.

"Good luck to you," called Uncle Donald. "Come back to see me at the end of the year."

When Huey reached the city, he found a carpenter to work for.

Huey worked for one year.

He learned to make tables and chairs.

When the time came for Huey to go home, the carpenter gave him a little wooden table.

"As long as you have this table," said the carpenter, "you will never be hungry. Just think of something delicious and say, TABLE SET!"

Huey closed his eyes
and thought of
something delicious.
Then he said, "TABLE SET!"

Suddenly there appeared on the table—
a baked turkey, fruit and candy, and
a delicious cherry pie.

The table was magic!

"Whatever you do," said the carpenter, "never let this table out of your sight!"

"I won't," said Huey. And he ate his cherry pie.

Then Huey thanked the carpenter, put the table on his back, and started home.

That night Huey stopped at The Old Inn.

"May I sleep here tonight?" he asked.

"Yes, you may," said the innkeeper. "But you are too late for dinner."

"That is all right," said Huey. "My magic table will give me dinner."

The innkeeper could not believe his ears.

So he peeked into Huey's room.

He heard Huey say, "TABLE SET!"

Suddenly there appeared on the table—
a big plate of spaghetti and meatballs.

"With a table like that," thought the innkeeper,
"I would never have to cook again."

And so when Huey was fast asleep,
the innkeeper sneaked into his room.

He took the magic table,
and left another table in its place.

In the morning Huey
put the table
on his back
and went home.

His uncle was glad to see him.

"Did you work hard?" he asked.

"Yes, Uncle Donald," said Huey. "But I will never have to work again. I have a magic table."

"There is no such thing as magic," said his uncle.

"Yes, there is," said Huey. "Watch!

"First I think of something delicious. Then I say, TABLE SET!"

Uncle Donald watched the table.

Nothing happened.

Again Huey said, "TABLE SET!"

This time a fly landed on the table.

"Is that what you call delicious?" asked Uncle Donald.

And he laughed and laughed.

Meanwhile, Dewey had gone to the country. There he found a farmer to work for.

Dewey stayed with him for one year.

He learned to grow corn and wheat.

When the time came for Dewey to go home, the farmer gave him a little donkey.

"As long as you have this donkey," said the farmer, "you will never be poor. Just think of how much money you want and say, DONKEY, DONKEY, WIGGLE YOUR EAR!"

Dewey closed his eyes and wished for ten gold coins.

Then he said, "DONKEY, DONKEY, WIGGLE YOUR EAR!"

Suddenly the donkey wiggled its ear and out came ten gold coins.

The donkey was magic!

"Whatever you do," said the farmer, "never let this donkey out of your sight."

"I won't," said Dewey.

Dewey put the coins in a bag.

Then he thanked the farmer, climbed on the donkey, and started home.

That night Dewey stopped at The Old Inn.

"All the rooms are taken," said the innkeeper. "But if you give me enough gold, you can sleep in the barn."

Dewey gave him his bag of gold coins.

"If that is not enough," said Dewey, "I can get more from my magic donkey."

“Just give me one more coin,” said the innkeeper.

He wanted to see what the donkey could do.

“DONKEY, DONKEY, WIGGLE YOUR EAR!” said Dewey.

A gold coin came falling out.

“I would be rich with a donkey like that,” thought the innkeeper.

And so when Dewey was fast asleep, the innkeeper sneaked into the barn.

He took the magic donkey away, and left another donkey in its place.

In the morning Dewey climbed on the donkey and rode home.

His uncle and brother came out to greet him.

"Did you work hard?" asked his uncle.

"Yes, Uncle Donald," said Dewey. "But I will never have to work again. I have a magic donkey."

"There is no such thing as magic," said his uncle.

"Yes, there is," said Dewey. "Watch! First I think of how much money I want. Then I say, DONKEY, DONKEY, WIGGLE YOUR EAR!"

His uncle watched the donkey.

All it did was kick up its heels.

"DONKEY, DONKEY, WIGGLE YOUR EAR!" shouted Dewey. But the donkey only swatted a fly with its tail.

The fly landed on Dewey's face.

"Is a fly what you wished for?" asked Uncle Donald.

And he laughed and laughed.

"That is strange," said Dewey.
"The magic worked at The Old Inn."

"That IS strange," said Huey.
"My magic table worked at The Old Inn, too."

"H-m-m-m-m," said the two brothers.

And while their uncle laughed and laughed, they thought and thought and thought.

Now Louie had gone to work in the woods.
There he lived with a woodcutter.
Louie helped him cut up logs for firewood.

One day a letter came.

Dear Louie,
Come home right away
The innkeeper at The Old Inn
is a thief.
He took a magic table
and a magic donkey from
us.
We must think of a way
to get them back.

Your two brothers

Louie told the woodcutter
that he had to go home right away.

"Here is a stick to take with you,"
said the woodcutter. "As long as you have it,
you will be safe. I will show you how it works."

Then the woodcutter said, "STICK, START BEATING ON THAT TREE."

The stick began to beat upon a tree—
RAT-A-TAT-TAT. RAT-A-TAT-TAT—
until the woodcutter told it to stop.

"This stick may be very useful," said Louie.
He thanked the woodcutter and started home.

When night came Louie stopped at The Old Inn.

"May I sleep here tonight?" he asked.

"Yes, you may," said the innkeeper. "Here, let me take that old stick."

"No," said Louie. "This is my magic stick. It keeps me safe!"

“H-m-m-m-m!” thought the innkeeper.
“I think I should have a magic stick.”

Late that night the innkeeper sneaked into Louie’s room.

He did not know that Louie was still awake.
He tried to take the magic stick.

Suddenly Louie cried, "STICK, START BEATING THAT THIEF!"

And the stick began to beat upon the innkeeper.

Up one arm and down the other.

RAT-A-TAT-TAT.

RAT-A-TAT-TAT.

Now in one place,
now another.

RAT-A-TAT-TAT.

RAT-A-TAT-TAT.

At last the innkeeper
cried, “Make it stop!
Make it stop!”

"Will you give me the magic table and the magic donkey that you stole from my brothers?" asked Louie.

"I will do anything!" cried the innkeeper.

"STICK, STOP BEATING!" said Louie. And the stick flew into his hand.

The next morning
Louie put the table
on the donkey's back.

Then he took his magic stick, climbed on the donkey, and rode home.

When Louie got home, his uncle and his brothers rushed out to greet him.

"Here is the magic table," he told them. "And here is the magic donkey. I got them with my magic stick."

"Magic, magic, magic!" cried Uncle Donald. "That is all you talk about.
But I have not seen any magic yet!"

"Uncle Donald, what would you like to eat?" asked Huey.

"A big slice of ice-cold watermelon," said his uncle.

So Huey said, "TABLE SET!"

Suddenly there appeared on the table four big slices of ice-cold watermelon.

One for each of them!

Then Dewey said, "Uncle Donald, how much gold would you like to have?"

"A great big pile of it!" said his uncle.

"DONKEY, DONKEY, WIGGLE YOUR EAR!" said Dewey.

The donkey wiggled and wiggled its ear, until—out came a great big pile of gold!

"Now, Uncle Donald," said Louie.
"Is there anything else you would like?"

"I would like to get rid of these flies!" cried his uncle.

"STICK, START BEATING!" said Louie.

And the magic stick began to swat the flies—
RAT-A-TAT-TAT. RAT-A-TAT-TAT—
until they were all gone.

Never again did Uncle Donald say there was no such thing as magic.